CAPTAIN FalSEBeaRD in A WILD GOOSE CHASE

FRED BLUNT

PUFFIN

Bristol Libraries

BRISTOL LIBRARIES
WITHDRAWN

1806378132

KT-149-958

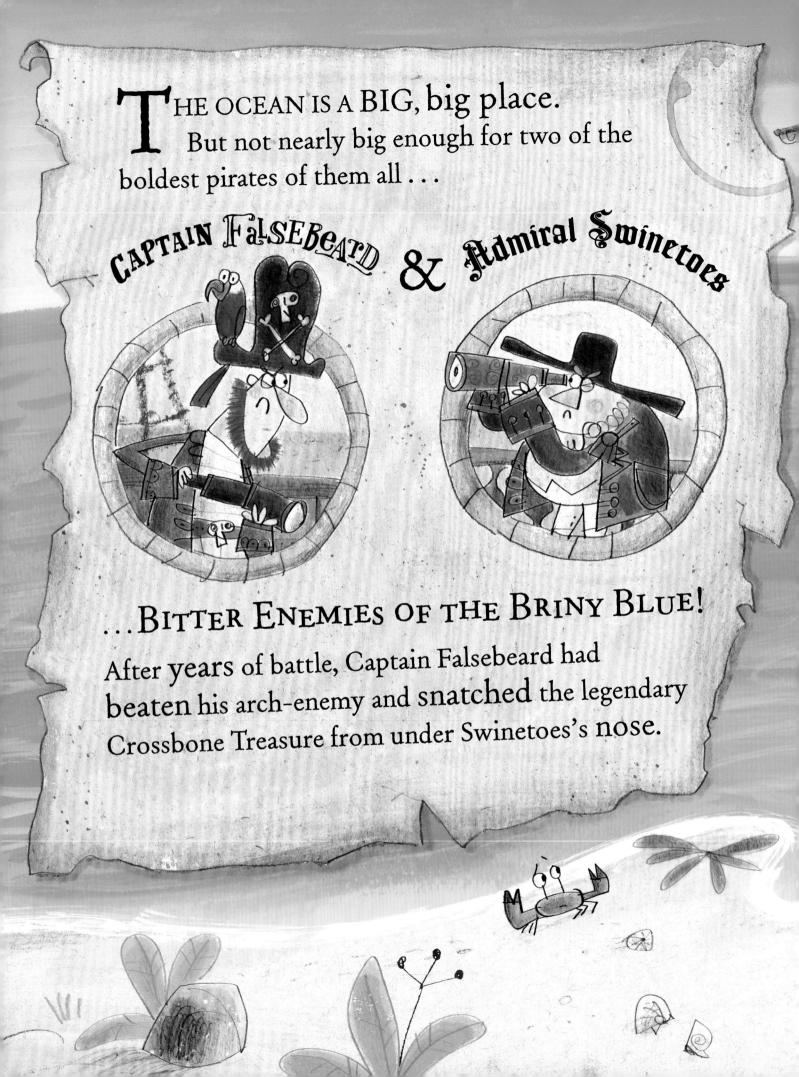

THE OCEAN IS A BIG, big place.
But not nearly big enough for two of the
boldest pirates of them all . . .

CAPTAIN FALSEBEARD & Admiral Swinetoes

. . . BITTER ENEMIES OF THE BRINY BLUE!

After years of battle, Captain Falsebeard had
beaten his arch-enemy and snatched the legendary
Crossbone Treasure from under Swinetoes's nose.

To celebrate their **victory**, Falsebeard and crew had anchored their ship, the *Pretty Polly* – with the treasure safely stored on-board – near a desert island. It was time to **relax** with a well-earned holiday.

The island life suited Captain Falsebeard down to the ground.

After a **busy** morning **sunbathing**, I reckon it be time for me afternoon **nap!**

The crew was delighted with their **riches**, and they spent each **lazy day** planning how to **spend** the fortune.

Driftwood Mac had his **eye** on a **new** accessory.

Yaar! I's gonna purchase me a **big old** pirate's **hat!**

While Big Tony fancied something a little more **permanent**.

I's gonna get me a **new** mermaid **tattoo**, right 'ere!

And the Seadog knew **exactly** what he wanted.

The happy pirates were having the **holiday** of a lifetime.
Little did they know that this was about to change . . .

Not so far away, a **dark** and dangerously **familiar** ship was lurking . . . Admiral Swinetoes's hateful galleon, the *Killjoy*!

At last, after weeks of searching, Swinetoes had discovered where Falsebeard and crew had hidden themselves – and the Crossbone Treasure.

The next day, Captain Falsebeard was just settling down for a spot of sunbathing when he spotted something strange in the sky.

As the bird flapped closer, there could be no mistaking that it was not a parrot at all but . . .

The goose dropped a **scroll** on to Falsebeard's head before landing on the beach and waddling away.

Falsebeard quickly got to his feet and opened the parchment.

As the crew assembled on the beach, Falsebeard cleared his throat and read from the scroll.

He who **catches** the GOLDEN goose will **reap** its GOLDEN egg!

Falsebeard was beside himself with excitement.
That goose had the ability to lay golden eggs?
That could mean only one thing . . .

TREASURE! TREASURE!

TREASURE!

Falsebeard wasted no time in sending the crew
to search the island and capture the bird.

Unfortunately, catching a goose was easier said than done.

The great chase took the crew ALL day . . .

and ALL over the island.

At long last, Captain Falsebeard began to close in . . .

. . . and captured the prize goose!

But, before the crew could celebrate, Big Tony spotted something.

And a pig's trotter could
only mean one thing . . .

SWINE TOES!

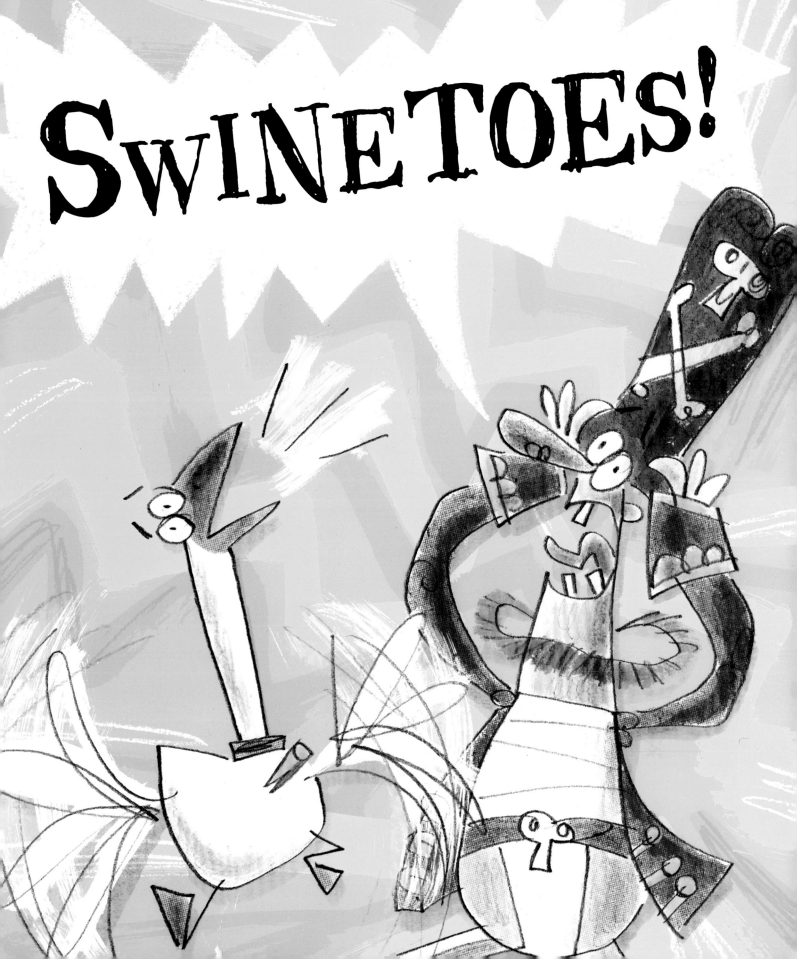

The great chase had been nothing but a distraction!
There would be no golden eggs, and when the crew returned
to the beach they saw that . . .

SWINETOES has STOLEN
the *Pretty Polly!*

Along with the precious
Crossbone Treasure!

Surrounded by **shark-infested** waters and soon to **run out** of food, they were in **deep trouble**. The crew **sank** to their knees in **despair**.

But Captain Falsebeard **refused** to give up. He knew the key to their **survival** was to keep **spirits** high and stay busy . . .

Quickly, the crew got to work, following the captain's orders. Driftwood Mac was sent to collect coconuts.

Flotsam and Jetsam built a **fire** to send up a smoke signal.

Big Tony tried to **convince** the goose to lay an egg for their supper.

Captain Falsebeard looked on, **pleased** with his crew's efforts.

The thought of years **stranded** on the island was too much for Big Tony. In a blind panic, the hungry pirate **dived** into the **sea** with an almighty **splash!**

But the **sharks** turned out to be . . .

The playful sea critters got Falsebeard thinking . . .

Now he knew **how** they could **beat** Swinetoes and **recapture** the treasure!

Sometime later, on-board the **captured** *Pretty Polly*, Admiral Swinetoes was **busy** telling the tale of his **revenge** over Captain Falsebeard.

Halfway through the **seventh** retelling, a **confused** shout came from the crow's nest.

Swinetoes was instantly SUSPICIOUS ...

That marooned **moron** won't fool me! Think you can send **dolphins** to attack us? Pah! **Think again!**

But, as the **dolphins** approached, they began to do something rather **strange** ...

While Swinetoes and his cohorts were
mesmerized by the dazzling dolphin display . . .

. . . Falsebeard and his crew **rode up** to the ship and climbed aboard.

They **tiptoed** across the deck and . . .

ushed Swinetoes and crew into the briny blue!

The waiting dolphins **flipped** the enemy pirates **high** into the air,

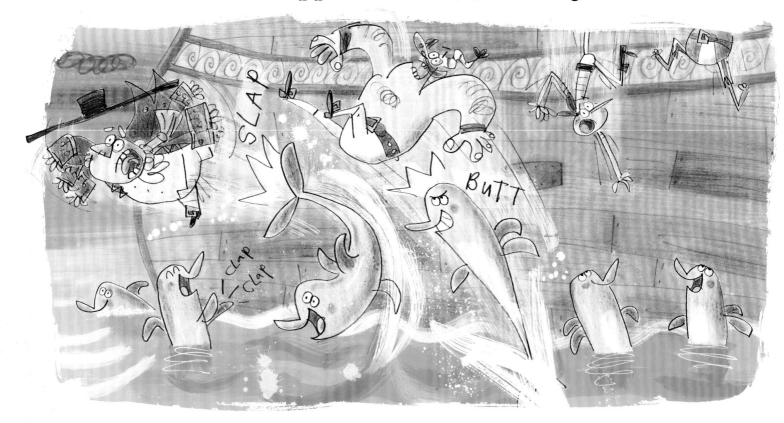

and **catapulted** them towards the desert island.

Sopping wet and **stranded**, with the *Killjoy* far away out at sea, Swinetoes could only watch as Falsebeard **sailed** past, reunited with the *Pretty Polly*, and the **precious** Crossbone Treasure.

Happy to be back home, Captain Falsebeard and his crew were in the mood to celebrate. The ship's cook rustled up a mighty feast, fit for the finest pirates to sail the seven seas!

THE END

(or is it . . . ?)

For Clarey, Bonnie and Sonny.
♥ My Treasures!
xxx

PUFFIN BOOKS
UK | USA | Canada | Ireland | Australia | India | New Zealand | South Africa
Puffin Books is part of the Penguin Random House group of companies
whose addresses can be found at global.penguinrandomhouse.com.
First published 2016
Text and illustrations copyright © Fred Blunt, 2016
The moral right of the author/illustrator has been asserted
A CIP catalogue record for this book is available from the British Library
Printed in China   001
ISBN: 978–0–723–29214–2